The Itty Bitty Kitten

by Liza Charlesworth

ISBN: 978-1-338-89035-8

Designer: Cynthia Ng; Illustrated by John Lund

Copyright © 2023 by Liza Charlesworth. All rights reserved. Published by Scholastic Inc.

1 2 3 4 5 6 7 8 9 10   68   31 30 29 28 27 26 25 24 23 22

Printed in Jiaxing, China. First printing, January 2023.

Meet a bear cub named Bob.
Meet his cat named Mittens.
Bob loved his pet a lot.
One day, something amazing happened....

Mittens had four cute kittens!
One was orange. One was gray.
One was striped. And one was
itty bitty with pretty spots.

Bob helped Mittens take care of her kittens.
He played with them. He cuddled them.
And when they were six weeks old,
Bob fed them special food.
The kittens grew and grew!

Then, one day, Bob's mom said,
"The kittens are eight weeks old.
It's time to find them nice new homes
in the neighborhood."
This news made Bob feel sad, but happy, too.

So Bob got out his markers
and made a big sign.
He posted the sign
in front of his house.

Bob was glad the kittens would
find nice new homes.
But he would miss them A LOT—
especially the itty bitty kitten.

Ding, dong! Bob's neighbor Jane
came by to meet the kittens.
She picked the orange one.
"I love taking care of pets!" she said.
Bob felt sad, but happy, too.

Ding, dong! Bob's neighbor Brad
came by to meet the kittens.
He picked the gray one.
"My whole family loves cats!" he said.
Bob felt sad, but happy, too.

Ding, dong! Bob's neighbor Kate
came by to meet the kittens.
She picked the striped one.
"My cat has always wanted a pal!" she said.
Bob felt sad, but happy, too.

Now, there was just one kitten left—
the itty bitty kitten with spots.
Bob played with it. Bob cuddled it.
Bob waited for the doorbell to ring.

But the doorbell did NOT ring.
In fact, a week went by and no one came.
"What if nobody picks the itty bitty kitten?"
Bob worried to his mom.
"How will it find a loving home?"

Bob's mom was quiet for a while.
Then, she said, "I was just about to tell you that
I found a VERY nice home for the last kitten."
"You did?" said Bob with surprise.
His tummy did a flip-flop.

"The VERY nice home is right here
with you and me and Mittens!"
"Really?" said Bob with excitement.

"Really!" said his mom with a smile.
This time, Bob did not feel sad at all—
only happy, happy, happy!

Then, Bob scooped up
the itty bitty kitten with spots.
And he gave it a great big cuddle.
Right here was the *PURR*-FECT
home indeed!